Rabén & Sjögren Bokförlag, Stockholm
www.raben.se

Translation copyright © 2007 by Rabén & Sjögren Bokförlag
All rights reserved
Originally published in Sweden by Rabén & Sjögren
under the title *En Flodhästsaga*
Copyright © 1993 by Lena Landström
Library of Congress Control Number: 2006928344
Printed in Denmark
First American edition, 2007

ISBN-13: 978-91-29-66603-8
ISBN-10: 91-29-66603-1

Lena Landström

A Hippo's Tale

Translated by Joan Sandin

R&S
BOOKS

Stockholm New York London Adelaide Toronto

Deep in the middle of Africa, a wide, dark river winds
through the thick jungle.

At a bend in the river is a nice muddy beach.
This is where the hippos live.

The big hippos enjoy relaxing in the nice warm water.

But the little hippos never hold still. They splash and play from morning till night. They like diving best of all.

Mrs. Hippopotamus lives alone, a little apart from the others.
She has just made a yummy seaweed pudding
for her dinner tonight.

While it is baking, she will take her evening bath.

Mrs. Hippopotamus has her own beach,
where she can bathe all alone, in peace and quiet.
The thick jungle grows all the way down to the water here,
and the muddy river bottom smells good.

But wait! What's this?
A monkey is fishing just off Mrs. Hippopotamus's private beach!
"I finally found a good place for night fishing," says the monkey.
"Don't let me disturb you if you're going to take a bath."

Mrs. Hippopotamus doesn't feel like bathing anymore.
She goes back home.

Her seaweed pudding doesn't taste very good.

Her bed isn't as soft and comfortable as it usually is.
Nothing feels right.

Suddenly she has an idea.
She's surprised she didn't think of it earlier.
A minute later, she is fast asleep.

The next morning, Mrs. Hippopotamus gets up early.
She must hurry or she won't be finished before evening.

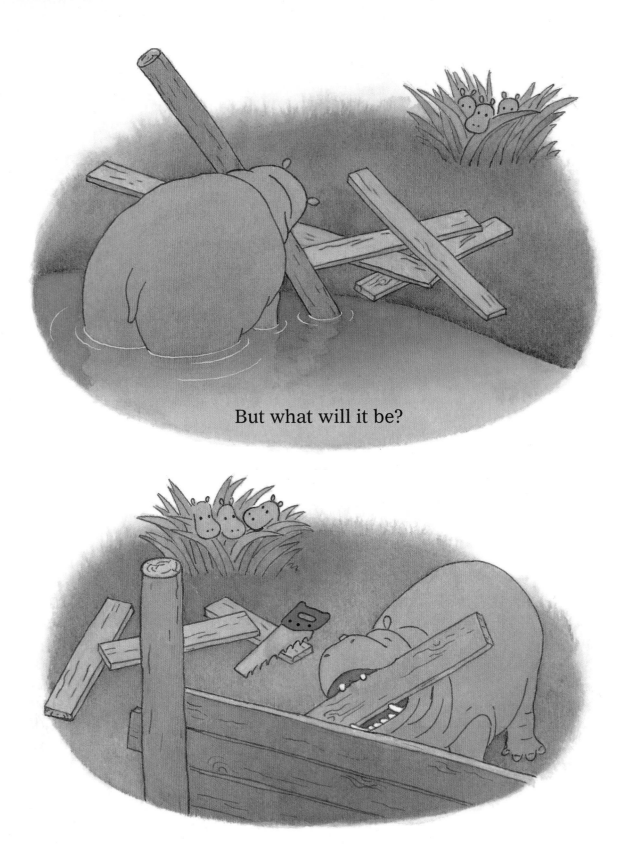

But what will it be?

A dock?

Or a boat?

"What is that thing?" asks the monkey. He has just arrived to fish.

"A BATHHOUSE," Mrs. Hippopotamus answers.

Mrs. Hippopotamus is pleased with her bathhouse. It has turned out exactly as she imagined it. But now she has to go home and make her seaweed pudding.

Mrs. Hippopotamus hums to herself as she whips up the pudding.

This will taste good after my evening bath, she thinks as she puts the piping-hot pudding in the window to cool.

But when she gets to the river, she is stopped in her tracks. "This is terrible!" she exclaims.

It seems just about everybody is at Mrs. Hippopotamus's beach, watching the little hippos dive from the top of her bathhouse.

She sighs and turns around.

On her way home, she stops by the big beach. It is completely empty.
She stands there for a moment thinking. She can hear the little
hippos playing and splashing over by her bathhouse.
"Well, there is nothing high for them to dive from here," she says
to herself.

Mrs. Hippopotamus takes her evening bath at the big beach.
Tomorrow, I'll build a diving board for them here, she decides.
Then she remembers the seaweed pudding . . .
Oh well, it will probably taste even better if it gets to
cool a little longer.